DUDLEY SCHOOLS LIBRARY
AND INFORMATION SERVICES

KU-798-616

Schools Library and Information Services

S00000679290

# ⌐FIRST GREEK MYTHS⌐
## THE SECRET OF PANDORA'S BOX

For Jake and Fleur Pirotta
*S.P.*

To my boys
*J.L.*

DUDLEY PUBLIC LIBRARIES

L 48036

679290 SCH

J292

Series reading consultant: Prue Goodwin, a lecturer in
Literacy in Education at the University of Reading

ORCHARD BOOKS
96 Leonard Street, London EC2A 4XD
*Orchard Books Australia*
32/45-51 Huntley Street, Alexandria, NSW 2015
This text was first published in Great Britain
in the form of a gift collection called *First Greek Myths*, in 2003
This edition first published in hardback in Great Britain in 2005
First paperback publication in 2006
Text © Saviour Pirotta 2005
Cover illustrations © Jan Lewis 2003
Inside Illustrations © Jan Lewis 2005
The rights of Saviour Pirotta to be identified as the author and
of Jan Lewis to be identified as the illustrator of this work
have been asserted by them in accordance with the
Copyright, Designs and Patents Act, 1988.
A CIP catalogue record for this book is available from the British Library.
ISBN 1 84362 809 0 (hardback)
ISBN 1 84362 781 7 (paperback)
1 3 5 7 9 10 8 6 4 2 (hardback)
1 3 5 7 9 10 8 6 4 2 (paperback)
Printed in Hong Kong, China
www.wattspublishing.co.uk

# ~FIRST GREEK MYTHS ~
## THE SECRET OF PANDORA'S BOX

## BY SAVIOUR PIROTTA
## ILLUSTRATED BY JAN LEWIS

ORCHARD BOOKS

# ~ CAST LIST ~

**PANDORA**
(Pan-door-a)

A beautiful woman and
a gift from the gods

**EPIMETHEUS**
(Epee-me-thee-us)

A good man

Long ago, at a time when the world was new, people lived happy and contented and there was no trouble or worry in the world.

Now there was a man called Epimetheus who had lots of friends but he longed for a wife to share his life.

One day, there was a knock
at Epimetheus's door. When he
opened it, a beautiful woman was
standing on his doorstep.

"My name is Pandora," said the woman. "The gods have sent me here to look after you."

"Why don't you come in?" said Epimetheus, smiling.

Inside the house, Pandora
looked around. It was a nice home
but it was in a mess. There was a
lot of work to be done.

She tidied up and washed the
dirty clothes.

Then she cooked a delicious
meal. Epimetheus was impressed.

"Where did you learn to cook like this?" Epimetheus asked.

Pandora smiled. "I don't know," she said. "I can't remember my past. All I know is that the gods sent me here to look after you."

Epimetheus couldn't help
thinking that it was all a bit strange,
but who was he to grumble about
having such a beautiful woman to
take care of him?

As Epimetheus ate, Pandora
went from room to room, opening
all the chests and cupboards.

"You are a very curious girl,"
said Epimetheus.

"I like to know where everything
is," said Pandora.

In the cellar she found more
chests but one looked different
from all the others. The wood was
very shiny and the lid was held
down with a rope.

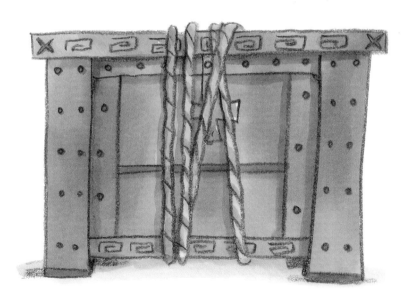

"Where did you get this
lovely chest?" Pandora
called up to Epimetheus.

"It was sent by the gods too,"
Epimetheus told her. "But
I was told never to open it."

14

"What is the point in having a chest that you can't open?" thought Pandora. "What on earth can be in it?"

Suddenly, Pandora thought she
could hear voices coming from
inside the chest.

"Pandora, help us, let us out,"
they seemed to be whispering.
Pandora was puzzled.

Then she heard a knock on the door upstairs. It was Epimetheus's brother.

"Come and meet Pandora," she heard Epimetheus say. "She was sent to me as a gift from the gods."

"Another gift from the gods?" said Epimetheus's brother. "Be careful, I think the gods may be trying to trick us."

"Why would they do that?" asked Epimetheus. "Pandora is not a trick! She is the best thing that has ever happened to me. Don't worry."

But perhaps poor Epimetheus should have worried. That night, Pandora lay awake. She was sure she could hear the voices calling to her from the chest in the cellar.

"Pandora, help us, let us out!"

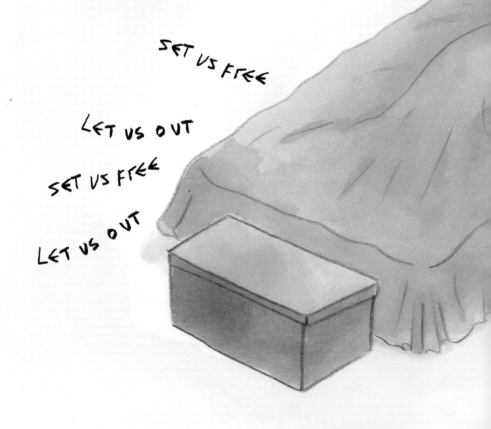

Pandora remembered what
Epimetheus had told her about not
opening the chest, but the voices
were getting louder and louder.

"Please, Pandora. Set us free!"

Slowly, silently, Pandora made
her way to the cellar.

"Just one little peep won't hurt,"
she said to herself. "Then I'll close
the chest again – for ever."

Carefully, she undid the rope and lifted the lid. There was laughter inside the chest, then the lid flew back and thousands of dark shadows swarmed into the cellar. They flitted around, buzzing and hissing.

The noise woke Epimetheus and
he ran downstairs to the cellar.

"Oh no!" he cried when he saw
the chest open and the shadows
flitting everywhere. "Pandora,
what have you done?"

"Something got out," whispered
Pandora. "It wasn't my fault. I
only opened the lid a little."

Epimetheus looked around him in horror. One of the shadows hissed, "I am Fear. These are all my brothers and sisters. We are curses sent by the gods to punish people for the wrongs that they do."

Pandora felt awful. But just then she noticed one tiny creature left inside the chest.

"Who are you?" asked Pandora.

"I am Hope," said the creature. "I sneaked into the box when the gods weren't looking. My job is to help undo the work of the nasty curses."

Gently, Pandora carried Hope outside and watched it flutter away on the air.

"Remember," Hope called back to Pandora. "Wherever there is trouble, I will be there to help."

Some people say that Hope is still flying around the world today, bringing help to those who need it.

# ~FIRST GREEK MYTHS~
## THE SECRET OF PANDORA'S BOX
BY SAVIOUR PIROTTA ⌐ ILLUSTRATED BY JAN LEWIS

❑ King Midas's Goldfingers     1 84362 804 X    £8.99

❑ Arachne, The Spider Woman     1 84362 805 8    £8.99

❑ The Secret of Pandora's Box     1 84362 809 0    £8.99

❑ Perseus and the Monstrous Medusa   1 84362 808 2    £8.99

❑ Icarus, The Boy Who Could Fly     1 84362 807 4    £8.99

❑ Odysseus and the Wooden Horse     1 84362 806 6    £8.99

## And enjoy a little magic with these First Fairy Tales:

❑ Cinderella     1 84121 138 9    £8.99

❑ Hansel and Gretel     1 84121 136 2    £8.99

❑ Jack and the Beanstalk     1 84121 134 6    £8.99

❑ Sleeping Beauty     1 84121 132 X    £8.99

❑ Rumpelstiltskin     1 84121 140 0    £8.99

❑ Snow White     1 84121 142 7    £8.99

❑ The Frog Prince     1 84362 456 7    £8.99

❑ Puss in Boots     1 84362 452 4    £8.99

First Greek Myths and First Fairy Tales are available from all
good bookshops,or can be ordered direct from the publisher:
Orchard Books, PO BOX 29, Douglas IM99 1BQ
Credit card orders please telephone 01624 836000
or fax 01624 837033
or e-mail: bookshop@enterprise.net for details.

To order please quote title, author and ISBN
and your full name and address.
Cheques and postal orders should be
made payable to 'Bookpost plc'.
Postage and packing is FREE within the UK
(overseas customers should add £1.00 per book).

Prices and availability are subject to change.